CARING FOR A PUPPY

For Jackson

First published 2013 by Devon Books.
www.devonthedog.com

Today our parents took us to buy a puppy.

We let him explore the yard.

Puppy was thirsty so we gave him a water bowl.

We gave him a collar so people knew he was ours.

He has lots of energy so we gave him a toy.

Then we threw a
ball for him.

After all that exercise Puppy was hungry so we gave him Puppy food.

Puppy needs to learn to do
his business outside.

Puppy was tired after his first
day so we gave him a bed.

As Puppy is older he can go to puppy school and learn how to behave.

Its good for him to interact
with other dogs to.

We also take Puppy to the park for walks.

Sometimes he swims in the river.

Then we need to wash him.

Puppy's fur is getting long and knotted so we need to brush him.

Puppy loves us…

...And we love Puppy!

Other Books from the same author and illustrator

DEVON THE DOG'S WILD ADVENTURE

Written and Illustrated
by Jonathan Short

www.devonthedog.com

"Do you eat bamboo like a panda?" asked Devon.

"Are you a polar bear that lives on the ice?" asked Devon. "No," said the baby.

About the Author

Jonathan Short is a young illustrator and children's book author. Recently completing a Graphic Design Degree, he has drawn cartoons for as long as he can remember. Jonathan has an interest in creating books for the early childhood age group with a focus on making the books fun and educational.

Devon the Dog is inspired by his first pet, a golden labrador named Max.

Devon the Dog Books can be purchased at www.devonthedog.com

Made in the USA
Middletown, DE
07 June 2021